THE BABYLON : DEMONS FAIRY AND GHOST

GOLU KUMAR

This book has been published with all efforts taken to make the material error-free after the consent of the author. However, the author and the publisher do not assume and hereby disclaim any liability to any party for any loss, damage, or disruption caused by errors or omissions, whether such errors or omissions result from negligence, accident, or any other cause.

While every effort has been made to avoid any mistake or omission, this publication is being sold on the condition and understanding that neither the author nor the publishers or printers would be liable in any manner to any person by reason of any mistake or omission in this publication or for any action taken or omitted to be taken or advice rendered or accepted on the basis of this work. For any defect in printing or binding the publishers will be liable only to replace the defective copy by another copy of this work then available.

Contents

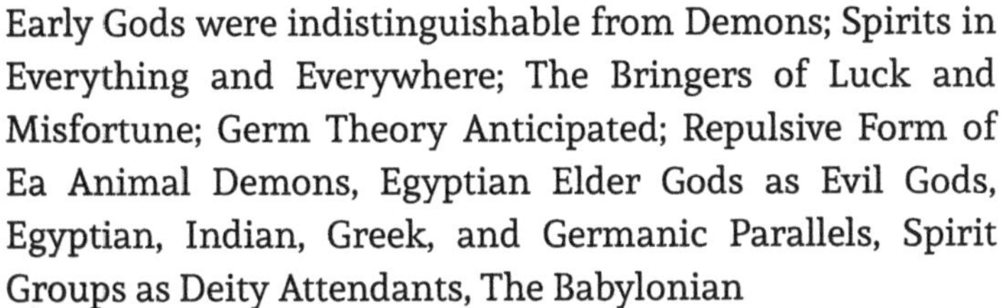

ONE

Early Gods were indistinguishable from Demons; Spirits in Everything and Everywhere; The Bringers of Luck and Misfortune; Germ Theory Anticipated; Repulsive Form of Ea Animal Demons, Egyptian Elder Gods as Evil Gods, Egyptian, Indian, Greek, and Germanic Parallels, Spirit Groups as Deity Attendants, The Babylonian

Elves and fairies, "Foreign Devils," "Will-o'-the-Wisp," "Demon Lovers," According to Children Charmed Against Evil Spirits, "Adam's first wife, Lilith" The Vengeful Dead Mother in Babylonia, India, Europe, and Mexico — The Demon of Nightmare — Ghosts as Enemies of the Living — Burial Contrast — Calling Back the Dead — Fate of Childless Ghosts —Religious Need for Children — Hags and Giants and Composite Monsters — Tempest Fiends — The Legend of Adapa and the Storm Demon — Ancient British Wind Hags — Tyrolean Storm Maidens — The Legend of the Zu Bird and the Indian Garuda Myth — The Legend of the Eagle and the Serpent — The Snake Mother Goddess — Demons and the Moon God — Plague Deities — Classification of Spirits — Parallels from Egyptian, Arabian, and Scottish Cultures

The memorable sermon preached by Paul to the Athenians when he stood "amid Mars' hill", could have been addressed with equal appropriateness to the ancient

Sumerians and Akkadians. "I perceive", he declared, "that in all things ye are too superstitious... God that made the world and all things therein, seeing that he is Lord of heaven and earth, dwelleth not in temples made with hands; neither is worshipped with men's hands as though he needed anything, seeing he giveth to all life, and breath and all things ... for in him we live, and move, and have our being; as certain also of your poets have said, For we are also his offspring. Forasmuch then as we are the offspring of God, we ought not to think that the Godhead is like unto gold, or silver, or stone, graven by art and man's device."[

Babylonian temples were houses of the gods in the literal sense; the gods were supposed to dwell in them, and their spirits had entered into the graven images or blocks of stone. It is probable that like the Ancient Egyptians they believed a god had as many spirits as he had attributes. The gods, as we have said, appear to have evolved from early spirit groups. All the world swarmed with spirits, which inhabited stones and trees, mountains and deserts, rivers and ocean, the air, the sky, the stars, and the sun and moon. The spirits controlled Nature: they brought light and darkness, sunshine and storm, summer and winter; they were manifested in the thunderstorm, the sandstorm, the glare of sunset, and the wraiths of mist rising from the steaming marshes. They controlled also the lives of men and women. The good spirits were the source of luck. The bad spirits caused misfortunes and were ever seeking to work evil against the Babylonians. Darkness was peopled by demons and ghosts of the dead. The spirits of disease were ever lying in wait to clutch him with cruel invisible hands.

Some modern writers, who are too prone to regard ancient peoples from a twentieth-century point of view, express grave doubts as to whether "intelligent

Babylonians" really believed that spirits came down in the rain and entered the soil to rise before men's eyes as stalks of barley or wheat. There is no reason for supposing that they thought otherwise. The early folks based their theories on the accumulated knowledge of their age. They knew nothing regarding the composition of water or the atmosphere, of the cause of thunder and lightning, or of the chemical changes effected in soils by the action of bacteria. They attributed all natural phenomena to the operations of spirits or gods. In believing that certain demons caused certain diseases, they may be said to have achieved distinct progress, for they anticipated the germ theory. They made discoveries, too, which have been approved and elaborated in later times when they lit sacred fires, bathed in sacred waters, and used oils and herbs to charm away spirits of pestilence. Indeed, many folk cures, which were originally associated with magical ceremonies, are still practiced in our day. They were found to be effective by early observers, although they were unable to explain why and how cures were accomplished, like modern scientific investigators.

In peopling the Universe with spirits, the Babylonians, like other ancient folks, betrayed that tendency to symbolize everything which has ever appealed to the human mind. Our painters and poets and sculptors are greatest when they symbolize their ideals and ideas and impressions, and by so doing make us respond to their moods. Their "beauty and their terror are sublime". But what may seem poetic to us, was invariably a grim reality to the Babylonians. The statue or picture was not merely a work of art but a manifestation of the god or demon. As has been said, they believed that the spirit of the god inhabited the idol; the frown of the brazen image was the frown of the wicked demon. They entertained as much dread of the winged and human-headed bulls guarding the entrance to the royal palace as do some of the Arab workmen who, in our day, assist excavators to rescue them from sandy mounds in which they have been hidden for long centuries.

When an idol was carried away from a city by an invading army, it was believed that the god himself had been taken prisoner, and was therefore unable any longer to help his people.

In the early stages of Sumerian culture, the gods and goddesses who formed groups were indistinguishable from demons. They were vaguely defined and had to change shapes. When attempts were made to depict them they were represented in many varying forms. Some were winged bulls or lions with human heads; others had even more remarkable composite forms. The "dragon of Babylon", for instance, which was portrayed on walls of temples, had a serpent's head, a body covered with scales, the fore legs of a lion, the hind legs of an eagle, and a long wriggling serpentine tail. Ea had several monster forms. The following description of one of these is repulsive enough:--

The head is the head of a serpent,
From his nostrils mucus trickles,
His mouth is beslavered with water;
The ears are like those of a basilisk,
His horns are twisted into three curls,
He wears a veil in his headband,
The body is such-fish full of stars,
The base of his feet are claws,
The sole of his foot has no heel,
His name is Sassu-winner,
A sea monster, a form of Ea.

Even after the gods were given beneficent attributes to reflect the growth of culture, and were humanized, they still retained many of their savage characteristics. Bel Enlil and his fierce son, Nergal, were destroyers of mankind; the storm god desolated the land; the sky god deluged it with rain; the sea raged furiously, ever hungering for human victims; the burning sun struck down its victims, and the floods played havoc with the dykes and houses of human beings. In Egypt, the sun god Ra was similarly a "producer of calamity", the composite monster god Sokar was "the lord of fear". Osiris in prehistoric times had been "a dangerous god", and some of the Pharaohs sought protection against him in the charms inscribed in their tombs. The Indian Shiva, "the Destroyer", in the old religious poems has also primitive attributes of like character.

The Sumerian gods never lost their connection with the early spirit groups. These continued to be represented by their attendants, who executed a deity's stern and vengeful decrees. In one of the Babylonian charms, the demons are referred to as "the spleen of the gods"--the symbols of their wrathful emotions and vengeful desires. Bel Enlil, the air and earth god was served by the demons of disease, "the beloved sons of Bel", which were issued from the Underworld to attack mankind. Nergal, the sulky and ill-tempered lord of death and destruction, who never lost his demoniac character, swept over the land, followed by the spirits of pestilence, sunstroke, weariness, and destruction. Anu, the sky god, had "spawned" at creation the demons of cold and rain and darkness. Even Ea and his consort, Damkina, were served by groups of devils and giants, which preyed upon mankind in bleak and desolate places when night fell. In the ocean home of Ea were bred the "seven evil spirits" of tempest--the gaping dragon, the leopard which preyed upon children, the great Beast, the terrible serpent, &c.

In Indian mythology, Indra was similarly followed by the stormy Maruts, and fierce Rudra by the tempestuous Rudras. In Teutonic mythology, Odin is the "Wild Huntsman in the Raging Host". In Greek mythology, the ocean furies attend to the fickle Poseidon. Other examples of this kind could be multiplied.

As we have seen (Chapter II) the earliest group of Babylonian deities consisted probably of four pairs of gods and goddesses as in Egypt. The first pair was Apsu-Rishta and Tiamat, who personified the primordial deep. Now the elder deities in most mythologies--the "grandsires" and "grandmothers" and "fathers" and "mothers"--are ever the most powerful and most vengeful. They appear to represent primitive "layers" of savage thought. The Greek Cronos devours even his children, and, as the late Andrew Lang has shown, there are many parallels to this myth among primitive peoples in various parts of the world.

Lang regarded Greek survival as an example of "the conservatism of the religious instinct". The grandmother of the Teutonic deity Tyr was a fierce giantess with nine hundred heads; his father was an enemy of the gods. In Scotland, the hag-mother of winter and storm and darkness is the enemy of growth and all life, and she raises storms to stop the grass from growing, to slay young animals, and prevent the union of her son with his fair bride. Similarly, the Babylonian chaos spirits, Apsu and Tiamat, the father and mother of the gods, resolve to destroy their offspring because they begin to set the Universe in order. Tiamat, the female dragon, is more powerful than her husband Apsu, who is slain by his son Ea. She summons to her aid the gods of evil and creates also a brood of monsters--serpents, dragons, vipers, fish men, raging hounds, &c.--to bring about universal and enduring confusion and evil. Not until she is destroyed can the beneficent gods establish law and order and make the earth habitable and beautiful.

But although Tiamat was slain, the everlasting battle between the forces of good and evil was ever waged in the Babylonian world. Certain evil spirits were let loose at certain periods, and they strove to accomplish the destruction of mankind and his works. These invisible enemies were either charmed away by performing magical ceremonies, or by invoking the gods to thwart them and bind them.

Other spirits inhabited the bodies of animals and were ever hovering near. The ghosts of the dead and male and female demons were birds, like the birds of Fate that sang to Siegfried. When the owl raised its melancholy voice in the darkness the listener heard the spirit of a departed mother crying for her child. Ghosts and evil spirits wandered through the streets in darkness; they haunted empty houses; they fluttered through the evening air as bats; they hastened, moaning dismally, across barren wastes searching for food or lay in wait for travelers; they came as roaring lions and howling jackals, hungering for human flesh. The "shed" was a destructive bull that might slay man wantonly or as a protector of temples. Of like character was the "lamassu", depicted as a winged bull with a human head, the protector of palaces; the "alu" was a bull-like demon of the tempest, and there were also many composites, distorted, or formless monsters which were vaguely termed "seizers" or "overthrowers", the Semitic "labashu" and "ach-crazy", the Sumerian "dimmer" and "dime-kur". A dialectic form of "gallu" or devil was "Mulla". Professor Pinches thinks it not improbable that "Mulla" may be connected with the word "Mula", meaning "star", and suggests that it referred to a "will-o'-the-wisp". In these islands, according to an old rhyme,

Some call him Robin Good-fellow,
Hob-goblin, or mad Crisp,
And some again doe tear me him oft
By name of Will the Wisp.

Other names are "Kitty", "Peg", and "Jack with a lantern". "Poor Robin" sang:

I should indeed as soon expect
That Peg-a-lantern would direct
Me straightway home on a misty night
As wandering stars, quite out of sight.

In Shakespeare's _Tempest_ a sailor exclaims: "Your fairy, which, you say, is a harmless fairy, has done little better than played the Jack with us". Dr. Johnson commented that the reference was to "Jack with a lantern". Milton wrote also of the "wandering fire",

Which of, they say, some evil spirit attends,
Hovering and blazing with delusive light,
Misleads th' amazing night wanderer from his way
To bogs and mires, and of through pond or pool;
There swallowed up and lost success far.

"When we stick in the mire", sang Drayton, "he doth with laughter leave us." These fires were also "fallen stars", "death fires", and "fire drakes":

So have I seen a fire drake glide along
Before a dying man, to point his grave,
And in it stick and hide.

Pliny referred to the wandering lights as stars.[87] The Sumerian "Mulla" was undoubtedly an evil spirit. In some countries the "fire drake" is a bird with a gleaming breast: in Babylonia, it assumed the form of a bull and may have had some connection with the bull of Ishtar. Like the Indian "Dasyu" and "Dasa",[88] Gallu was applied in the sense of "foreign devil" to human and superhuman adversaries of certain monarchs. Some of the supernatural beings resemble our elves and fairies and the Indian Rakshasas. Occasionally they appear in comely human guise; at other times they are vaguely monstrous. The best known of this class is Lilith, who, according to Hebrew tradition, preserved in the Talmud, was the demon lover of Adam. She has been immortalized by Dante Gabriel Rossetti:

Of Adam's first wife Lilith, it is told
(The witch he loved before the gift of Eve)
That, ere the snake's, her sweet tongue could deceive,
And her enchanted hair was the first gold.
And still, she sits, young while the earth is old,
And, subtly of herself contemplative,
Draws men to watch the bright web she can weave,
Till heart and body and life are in its hold.
The rose and poppy are her flowers; for where
Is he not found, O Lilith, who shed scent
And soft shed kisses and soft sleep shall snare?
Lo! as that youth's eyes burned at thin, so went
Thy spell through him, and left his straight neck bent
And round his heart one strangling golden hair.

Lilith is the Babylonian Lilith, a feminine form of Lilu, the Sumerian Lila. She resembles Surpanakha of the _Ramayana_, who made love to Rama and Lakshmana, and the sister of the demon Hidimva, who became enamored of Bhima, one of the heroes of the _Mahabharata_,[89] and the various fairy lovers of Europe who lured men to eternal imprisonment inside mountains, or vanished forever when they were completely under their influence, leaving them demented. The elfin Lilu similarly wooed young women, like the Germanic Laurin of the "Wonderful Rose Garden",[90] who carried away the fair lady Kunhild to his underground dwelling amidst the Tyrolese mountains, or left them haunting the place of their meetings, searching for him in vain:

A savage place! as holy and enchanted
As are beneath the waning moon was haunted
By woman wailing for her demon lover...
His flashing eyes, his floating hair!
Weave a circle around him thrice,
And close your eyes with holy dread,
For he on honey-dew hath fed
And drunk the milk of Paradise.

Another materializing spirit of this class was Ardat Lili, who appears to have wedded human beings like the swan maidens, the mermaids, and Nereids of the European folk tales, and the goddess Ganga, who for a time was the wife of King Shantanu of the _Mahabharata_.

The Labartu, to whom we have referred, was a female who haunted mountains and marshes; like the fairies and hags of Europe, she stole or afflicted children, who accordingly had to wear charms round their necks for protection. Seven of these supernatural beings were reputed to be daughters of Anu, the sky god.

The Alu, a storm deity, was also a spirit that caused nightmares. It endeavored to smother sleepers like the Scandinavian hag Mara and similarly deprived them of the power to move. In Babylonia, this evil spirit might also cause sleeplessness or death by hovering near a bed. In shape, it might be as horrible and repulsive as the Egyptian ghosts which caused children to die from fright or by sucking out the breath of life.

As most representatives of the spirit world were enemies of the living, so were the ghosts of dead men and women. Death chilled all human affections; it turned love to hate;

the deeper the love had been, the deeper became the enmity fostered by the ghost. Certain ghosts might also be regarded as particularly virulent and hostile if they happened to have left the body of one who was ceremonially impure. The most terrible ghost in Babylonia was that of a woman who had died on a childbed. She was pitied and dreaded; her grief had demented her; she was doomed to wail in the darkness; her impurity clung to her like poison. No spirit was more prone to work evil against mankind, and her hostility was accompanied by the most tragic sorrow. In Northern India the Hindus, like the ancient Babylonians, regard as a fearsome demon the ghost of a woman who died while pregnant, or on the day of the child's birth.[92] A similar belief prevailed in Mexico. In Europe, there are many folk tales of dead mothers who return to avenge themselves on the cruel fathers of neglected children.

A sharp contrast is presented by the Mongolian Buriats, whose outlook on the spirit world is less gloomy than that of the ancient Babylonians. According to Mr. Jeremiah Curtin, these interesting people are wont to perform a ceremony with the purpose to entice the ghost to return to the dead body--a proceeding which is dreaded in the Scottish Highlands.[93] The Buriats address the ghost, saying: "You shall sleep well. Come back to your natural ashes. Take pity on your friends. It is necessary to live a real life. Do not wander along the mountains. Do not be like bad spirits. Return to your peaceful home... Come back and work for your children. How can you leave the little ones?" If it is a mother, these words have great effect; sometimes the spirit moans and sobs, and the Buriats tell that there have been instances of it returning to the body.[94] In his _Arabia Deserta_[95] Doughty relates that Arab women and children mock the cries of the owl. One explained to him: "It is a wailful woman seeking her lost child; she has become this forlorn bird". So do immemorial beliefs survive to our day?

The Babylonian ghosts of unmarried men and women and those without offspring were also disconsolate night wanderers. Others who suffered similar fates were the ghosts of men who died in battle far from home and were left unburied, the ghosts of travelers who perished in the desert and were not covered over, the ghosts of drowned men who rose from the water, the ghosts of prisoners starved to death or executed, the ghosts of people who died violent deaths before their appointed time. The dead required to be cared for, to have libations poured out, to be fed so that they might not prowl through the streets or enter houses searching for scraps of food and pure water. The duty of giving offerings to the dead was imposed apparently on near relatives. As in India, it would appear that the eldest son performed the funeral ceremony: a dreadful fate, therefore, awaited the spirit of the dead Babylonian man or woman without offspring. In Sanskrit literature, there is a reference to a priest who was not allowed to enter Paradise, although he had performed rigid penances because he had no children.[96]

There were hags and giants of mountain and desert, of river and ocean. Demons might possess the pig, the goat, the horse, the lion, or the ibis, the raven, or the hawk. The seven spirits of tempest, fire, and destruction rose from the depths of the ocean, and there were hosts of demons that could not be overcome or baffled by man without the assistance of the gods to whom they were hostile. Many were sexless; having no offspring, they were devoid of mercy and compassion. They penetrated everywhere:

The high enclosures, the broad enclosures, like a flood they pass through,
From house to house they dash along.
No door can shut them out;
No bolt can turn them back.
Through the door, like a snake, they glide,
Through the hinge, like the wind, they storm,
Tearing the wife from the embrace of the man,
Driving the freedman from his family home.[97]

These furies did not confine their unwelcomed attention to mankind alone:

They hunt the doves from their cotes,
And drive the birds from their nests,
And chase the marten from its hole...
Through the gloomy street by night, they roam,
Smiting sheepfold and cattle pen,
Shutting up the land as with door and bolt.

The Babylonian poet, like Burns, was filled with pity for the animals which suffered in the storm:

Listening to the doors an' windsocks rattle,
I thought me o' the ourie cattle,
Or silly sheep, wha bide this brattle
O' winter war...
Ilk happing bird, wee, helpless thing!
That is the merry months o' spring
Delighted me to hear thee sing,
What comes o' thee?
Whore wilt thou cow's thy chittering wing,
And close thy eye?

According to Babylonian belief, "the great storms directed from heaven" were caused by demons. Mankind heard them "loudly roaring above, gibbering below".[98] The south wind was raised by Shutu, a plumed storm demon resembling Hraesvelgur of the Icelandic Eddas:

Corpse-swallower sits at the end of heaven,
A Jötun in eagle form;
From his wings, they say, comes the wind which fares
Overall the dwellers of earth.[99]

The northern story of Thor's fishing, when he hooked and wounded the Midgard serpent, is recalled by the Babylonian legend of Adapa, son of the god Ea. This hero was engaged in catching fish, when Shutu, the south wind, upset his boat. In his wrath, Adapa immediately attacked the storm demon and shattered her pinions. Anu, the sky god, was moved to anger against Ea's son and summoned him to the Celestial Court. Adapa, however, appeared in garments of mourning and was forgiven. Anu offered him the water of life and the bread of life which would have made him immortal, but Ea's son refused to eat or drink, believing, as his father had warned him, that the sky god desired him to partake of the bread of death and to drink of the water of death.

Another terrible atmospheric demon was the southwest wind, which caused destructive storms and floods, and claimed many human victims like the Icelandic "corpse swallower". She was depicted with lidless staring eyes, a broad flat nose, a mouth gaping horribly, and showing tusk-like teeth, and with high cheekbones, heavy eyebrows, and a low bulging forehead.

In Scotland, the hag of the southwest wind is similarly a bloodthirsty and fearsome demon. She is most virulent in the springtime. At Cromarty, she is quaintly called "Gentle Annie" by the fisher folks, who repeat the saying: "When Gentle Annie is skyawlan (yelling) round the heel of Ness (a promontory) wi' a white feather on her hat (the foam of big billows) they (the spirits) will be harrying (robbing) the crook"--that is, the pot which hangs from the crook is empty during the spring storms, which prevent fishermen going to sea. In England, the wind hag is Black Annis, who dwells in a Leicestershire hill cave. She may be identical to the Irish hag Anu, associated with the "Paps of Anu". According to Gaelic lore, this wind demon of spring is the "Cailleach" (old wife). She gives her name in the Highland calendar to the stormy period of late spring; she raises gale after gale to prevent the coming of summer. Angerboda, the Icelandic hag, is also a storm demon but represents the east wind. A Tyrolese folk tale tells of three magic maidens who dwelt on Jochgrimm mountain, where they "brewed the winds". Their demon lovers were Ecke, "he who causes fear"; Vasolt, "he who causes dismay"; and the scornful Dietrich in his mythical character of Donar or Thunor (Thor), the thunderer.

Another Sumerian storm demon was the Zu bird, which is represented among the stars by Pegasus and Taurus. A legend relates that this "worker of evil, who raised the head of evil", once aspired to rule the gods, and stole from Bel, "the lord" of deities, the Tablets of Destiny, which gave him his power over the Universe as controller of the fates of all. The Zu bird escaped with the Tablets and found shelter on its mountain top in Arabia. Anu called on Ramman, the thunderer, to attack the Zu bird, but he was afraid; other gods appear to have shrunk from the conflict. How the rebel was overcome is not certain, because the legend survives in fragmentary form. There is a reference, however, to the moon god setting out towards the mountain in Arabia with a purpose to outwit the Zu bird and recover the lost Tablets. How he fared it is impossible to ascertain. In another legend--that of Etana--the mother serpent, addressing the sun god, Shamash, says:

Thy net is like unto the broad earth; Thy snare is like unto the distant heaven! Who hath ever escaped from thy net? Even Zu, the worker of evil, who raised the head of evil [did not escape]!

In Indian mythology, Garuda, half giant, half eagle, robs the Amrita (ambrosia) of the gods which gives them their power and renders them immortal. It had assumed a golden body, bright as the sun. Indra, the thunderer, flung his bolt in vain; he could not wound Garuda, and only displaced a single feather. Afterward, however, he stole the moon goblet containing the Amrita, which Garuda had delivered to his enemies, the serpents, to free his mother from bondage. This Indian eagle giant became the vehicle of the god Vishnu, and, according to the _Mahabharata_, "mocked the wind with his fleetness".

It would appear that the Babylonian Zu bird symbolized the summer sandstorms from the Arabian desert. Thunder is associated with the rainy season, and it may have been assumed, therefore, that the thunder god was powerless against the sandstorm demon, who was chased, however, by the moon, and finally overcome by the triumphant sun when it broke through the darkening sand drift and brightened heaven and earth, "netting" the rebellious demon who desired to establish the rule of evil over gods and mankind.

In the "Legend of Etana" the Eagle, another demon that links with the Indian Garuda, a slayer of serpents, devours the brood of the Mother Serpent. For this offense against divine law, Shamash, the sun god, pronounces the Eagle's doom. He instructs the Mother Serpent to slay a wild ox and conceal herself in its entrails. The Eagle comes to feed on the carcass, unheeding the warning of one of his children, who says, "The serpent lies in this wild ox":

He swooped down and stood upon the wild ox,
The Eagle ... examined the flesh;
He looked about carefully before and behind him;
He again examined the flesh;
He looked about carefully before and behind him,
Then, moving swiftly, he made for the hidden parts.
When he entered into the midst,
The serpent seized him by his wing.

In vain the Eagle appealed for mercy to the Mother Serpent, who was compelled to execute the decree of Shamash; she tore off the Eagle's pinions, wings, and claws, and threw him into a pit where he perished from hunger and thirst.[100] This myth may refer to the ravages of a winged demon of disease who was thwarted by the sacrifice of an ox. The Mother Serpent appears to be identical to an ancient goddess of maternity resembling the Egyptian Bast, the serpent mother of Bubastis. According to Sumerian belief, Nintu, "a form of the goddess Ma", was half a serpent. On her head there is a horn; she is "girt about the loins"; her left arm holds "a babe suckling her breast":

From her head to her loins The body is that of a naked woman; From the loins to the sole Scales like those of a snake are visible.

The close association of gods and demons is illustrated in an obscure myth which may refer to an eclipse of the moon or a night storm at the beginning of the rainy season. The demons go to war against the high gods and are assisted by Adad (Ramman) the thunderer, Shamash the sun, and Ishtar. They desire to wreck the heavens, the home of Anu:

They clustered angrily around the crescent of the moon god,
And won over to their aid Shamash, the mighty, and Adad,

the
Warrior,
And Ishtar, who with Anu, the King,
Hath founded a shining dwelling.

The moon god Sin, "the seed of mankind", was darkened by the demons who raged, "rushing lose over the land" like the wind. Bel called upon his messenger, whom he sent to Ea in the ocean depths, saying: "My son Sin ... hath been grievously bedimmed". Ea lamented, and dispatched his son Merodach to net the demons by magic, using "a two-colored cord from the hair of a virgin kid and the wool of a virgin lamb".

As in India, where Shitala, the Bengali goddess of smallpox, for instance, is worshipped when the dreaded disease she controls becomes epidemic, so in Babylonia, the people sought to secure immunity from attack by worshipping spirits of disease. A tablet relates that Ura, a plague demon, once resolved to destroy all life, but ultimately consented to spare those who praised his name and exalted him in recognition of his bravery and power. This could be accomplished by reciting a formula. Indian serpent worshippers believe that their devotions "destroy all danger proceeding from snakes".

Like the Ancient Egyptians, the Babylonians also had their kindly spirits who brought luck and the various enjoyments of life. A good "labor" might attend to a human being like a household fairy of India or Europe: a friendly "she" could protect a household against the attacks of fierce demons and human enemies. Even the spirits of Fate who served Anu, god of the sky, and that "Norn" of the Underworld, Eresh-ki-gal, queen of Hades, might sometimes be propitious: if the deities were successfully invoked they could cause the Fates to smite spirits of disease and bringers of ill luck. Damu, a friendly fairy goddess, was well loved, because she inspired pleasant dreams, relieved the sufferings of the afflicted, and restored to good health those patients whom she selected to favor.

In the Egyptian _Book of the Dead_ the kindly spirits are overshadowed by the evil ones because the various magical spells which were put on record were directed against those supernatural beings who were enemies of mankind. Similarly in Babylonia the fragments of this class of literature that survive deal mainly with wicked and vengeful demons. It appears probable, however, that the highly emotional Sumerians and Akkadians were on occasion quite as cheerful a people as the inhabitants of ancient Egypt. Although they were surrounded by bloodthirsty furies who desired to shorten their days, and their nights were filled with vague lowering phantoms that inspired fear, they no doubt shared, in their charm-protected houses, a comfortable feeling of security after performing magical ceremonies, and were happy enough when they gathered round flickering lights to listen to ancient song and story and gossip about crops and traders, the members of the royal house, and the family affairs of their acquaintances.

The Babylonian spirit world, it will be seen, was complex. Its inhabitants were numberless, but often vaguely defined, and one class of demons linked with another. Like the European fairies of folk belief, the Babylonian spirits were extremely hostile and irresistible at certain seasonal periods; and they were fickle and perverse and difficult to please even when inclined to be friendly. They were also similarly manifested from time to time in various forms. Sometimes they were comely and beautiful; at other times they were apparitions of horror. The Jinn of present-day Arabians are like; these may be giants, cloudy shapes, comely women, serpents or cats, goats or pigs.

Some of the composite monsters of Babylonia may suggest the vague and exaggerated recollections of terror-stricken people who have had glimpses of unfamiliar wild beasts in the dusk or amidst reedy marshes. But they cannot be wholly accounted for in this way. While animals were often identified with supernatural beings, and foreigners were called "devils", it would be misleading to assert that the spirit world reflects confused folk memories of human and bestial enemies. Even when a demon was given concrete human form it remained essentially non-human: no ordinary weapon could inflict an injury, and it was never controlled by natural laws. The spirits of disease and tempest and darkness were creations of fancy: they symbolized moods; they were the causes that explained effects. A sculptor or storyteller who desired to convey an impression of a spirit of storm or pestilence created monstrous forms to inspire terror. Sudden and unexpected visits of fierce and devastating demons were accounted for by asserting that they had wings like eagles, were nimble-footed as gazelles, cunning and watchful as serpents; that they had claws to clutch, horns to gore, and powerful fore legs like a lion to smite down victims. Withal they drank blood like ravens and devoured corpses like hyaenas. Monsters were all the more repulsive when they were part human. The human-headed snake or the snake-headed man and the man with the horns of a wild bull and the legs of a goat were horrible in the extreme. Evil spirits might sometimes achieve success by practicing deception. They might appear as beautiful girls or handsome men and seize unsuspecting victims in deathly embrace or leave them demented and full of grief or come as birds and suddenly assume awesome shapes.

Some people consider fairies, elves, and other half-human demons to be corrupt gods. It will be clear, though, that although some spirits evolved into gods, others stayed somewhere in between these two categories of supernatural beings. They might serve gods and goddesses, or they might act on their own now to wage war against humans and even deities. For instance, the "namtaru" was a spirit of destiny who was the child of the Hades queen Eresh-ki-gal and Bel-Enlil. According to Professor Pinches, "it appears that he carried out the directives given to him regarding the fate of mortals, and could also have authority over some of the gods." [103] The bad gods that rebelled against the good gods belong to this middle class. The fallen angels are classified into three groups in Hebridean folklore: the fairies, the "nimble men" (aurora borealis), and the "blue men of the Minch." The "brood of Cain" in Beowulf includes "monsters, elves, sea-devils, and giants as well, who long battled with God, for which he gave them their reward." [104] Similar to this, the spirit groupings of Babylon are subject to division and subdivision. The various classes can be seen as remnants of the several stages of development, from primitive animism to sublime monotheism; in the incomplete narratives, we can see the floating elements that have formed the basis of vast myths.

9 798887 831732

Printed by Libri Plureos GmbH in Hamburg,
Germany